the world of
ERiC CARLE™

My First Sticker Treasury

This edition published by Parragon Books Ltd in 2016 and distributed by

Parragon Inc.
440 Park Avenue South, 13th Floor
New York, NY 10016
www.parragon.com

ISBN 978-1-4748-3041-6

Printed in China

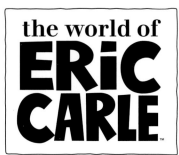

the world of
**ERiC
CARLE**™

Welcome to your sticker treasury.

Read the fun facts in each chapter and add your animal stickers to finish the pages. You'll find your stickers at the back of the book.

Happy stickering!

PaRRagon

Bath · New York · Cologne · Melbourne · Delhi
Hong Kong · Shenzhen · Singapore

CONTENTS

Forests

Forests are filled with trees
and wildlife. During autumn, animals
stock up on fruits and seeds to get
ready for a cold winter.

Rabbits and Hares

Rabbits and **hares** look similar, but they have different habits. Most rabbits live underground whereas hares live above the ground. Hares can run much faster, too.

Boing! Boing!

Rabbits have strong back legs—perfect for hopping!

A hare is bigger than a rabbit. It has a larger body and longer legs.

Long ears help a rabbit listen for danger.

Did you know?

A rabbit has eyes on the side of its head. It can see what is happening behind it, without turning around!

Butterflies

Butterflies have beautiful, colorful wings. Most butterflies like to live in warm places.

The **blue morpho** is one of the largest butterflies in the world.

The **monarch butterfly** flies thousands of miles to find somewhere warm to live.

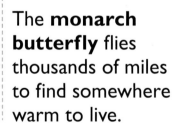

The wings make a fluttering sound when the butterfly flies.

Deer

Deer live in big groups called herds. They have short, brown fur to keep them warm.

A baby deer is called a fawn.

Reindeer live in cold countries. They use their antlers to push away snow to find tasty plants.

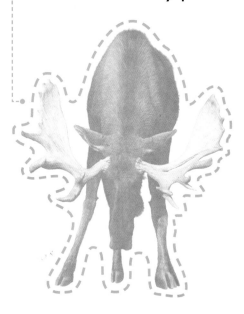

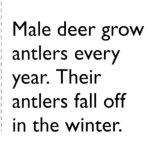

Male deer grow antlers every year. Their antlers fall off in the winter.

Birds and Beetles

Forests are the perfect home for **birds** and **beetles**. Birds make nests high up in the trees, and beetles chew on tree bark.

The **northern cardinal** is a songbird. Its musical tweets sound like a song.

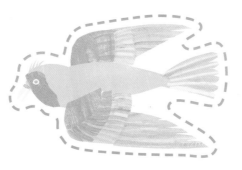

Woodpeckers peck holes in tree trunks to find food.

Beetles use their long jaws to fight each other.

Did you know?

Stag beetles can fly!

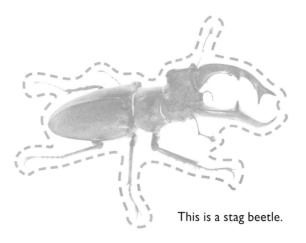

This is a stag beetle.

Bears

Bears are strong and have big claws that they use to dig cozy dens, which keep the bears warm in the winter.

A grizzly bear is a type of brown bear.

Grizzly bears usually give birth to twins.

Did you know?
Bears are great at swimming and catching fish.

A baby bear is called a **cub**.

Can you color in this bear?

Panda Bears

Panda bears have black rings of fur around their eyes. They like to live alone in bamboo forests.

A baby panda is born in a tree hollow or a rocky cave.

Pandas can climb high up into the trees.

A newborn panda is smaller than a mouse!

Pandas spend most of their day eating bamboo.

OCEANS

The oceans cover almost three quarters of the planet. They are home to billions of creatures, including the largest animal on Earth, the blue whale.

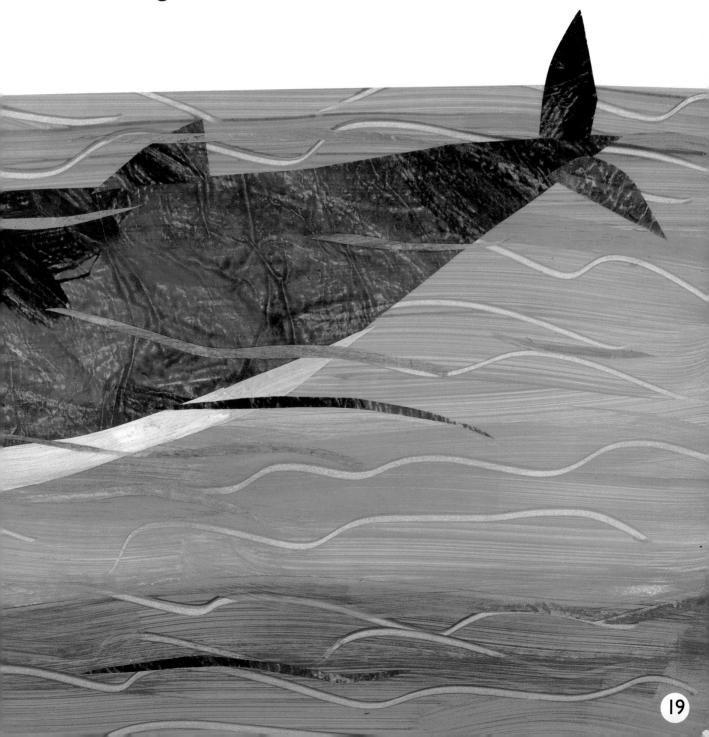

Fish

There are lots of different types of **fish** in the ocean. They can can breathe underwater and most fish have scales on their bodies.

Fish have fins to help them swim.

A **stonefish** can shoot a deadly poison from its spines.

A shark is a type of fish.

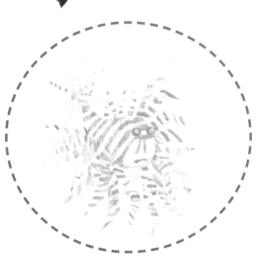

A **lionfish** can sting humans with its fins.

This is a lionfish.

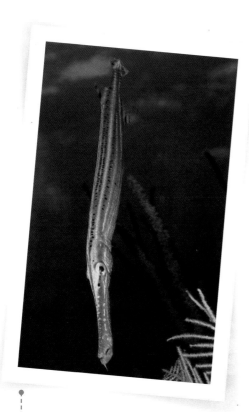

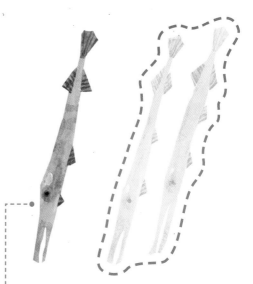

Trumpetfish often swim with their heads pointing down.

Trumpetfish have long bodies and snouts. They look a bit like sticks or weeds on the ocean floor.

Did you know?

Trumpetfish can change color.

Pipefish don't have fins, so they are very slow swimmers.

This is a pipefish.

Fish Babies

Fish lay eggs in the ocean or on the ocean floor. The eggs then hatch into **baby fish**.

Here are some fish eggs.

A male bullhead catfish with his baby fish.

Some baby fish hide among the tentacles of **jellyfish**!

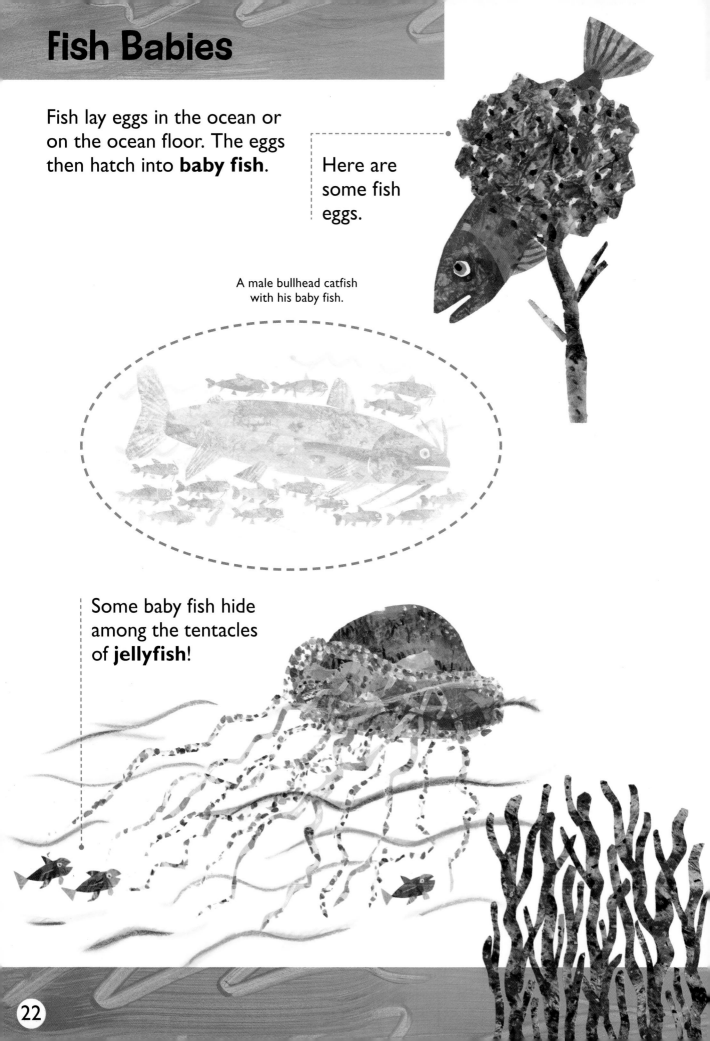

Seabirds

Seabirds make nests on rocky cliffs. When they are hungry, the birds fly over the oceans to find fish to eat.

The **bald eagle** uses its strong claws to catch fish.

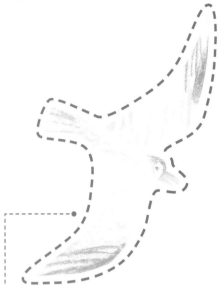

Seagulls aren't scared of humans. They sometimes steal picnics on the beach!

The **Australian pelican** has the longest beak in the world.

Can you color in this pelican?

Seahorses

A **seahorse** is a type of fish. Its head looks like a horse's head!

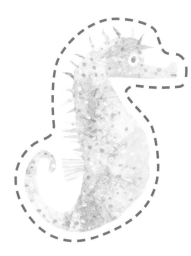

These seahorses are clinging to the coral with their tails.

The female puts her eggs into a special pouch on the male's body.

The male seahorse carries the eggs in his pouch, until the eggs hatch.

Did you know?

Seahorses are the slowest swimmers in the ocean.

Lots of baby seahorses swim out of the pouch. Goodbye, little ones!

The **weedy seadragon** looks like it's covered in leaves. It is great at hiding in the weeds.

25

Whales

Whales are mammals. They cannot breathe underwater like fish— they come to the surface to take breaths of air.

The **blue whale** is the largest mammal on Earth.

Did you know?

Some whales sing to each other.

A whale breathes through a blowhole on the top of its body.

Dolphins

Dolphins are playful mammals. They ride the waves of the ocean and call to each other using squeaks and whistles.

A group of dolphins is called a pod.

Dolphins can jump high out of the water. They could jump over a giraffe!

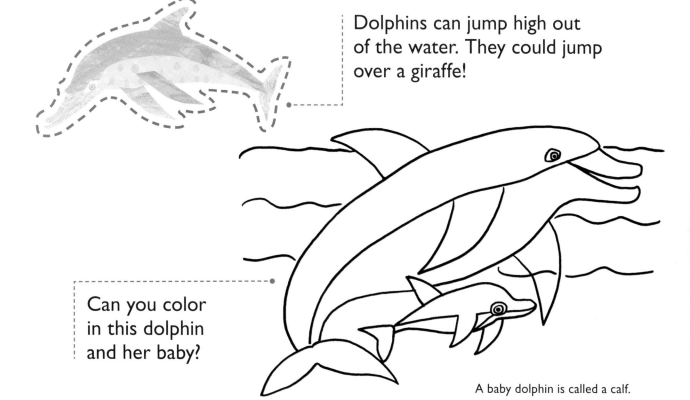

Can you color in this dolphin and her baby?

A baby dolphin is called a calf.

Lobsters and Octopuses

Lobsters have hard shells to protect them, but **octopuses** are soft—they can squeeze through a space as tiny as a coin.

Lobsters have huge claws.

A lobster's teeth are in its stomach!

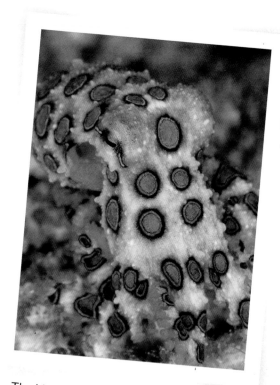

The blue-ringed octopus has a poisonous bite.

An octopus can taste and smell with the suckers on its eight tentacles.

Turtles

A **turtle's** back is covered by a hard shell —it is like a shield to keep the turtle safe.

Green turtles lay their eggs on the beach.

Turtles hide inside their shells if they are in danger.

This is a leatherback turtle.

Turtles are great swimmers. A **leatherback turtle** once swam halfway around the world!

Grasslands

Grasslands are found all over the world, from Europe and Asia to North and South America. African grasslands, called savannahs, are home to a dazzling collection of animals, including the lion.

Zebras

Zebras are part of the horse family, but their striped coats make them look very different. Their coats help zebras to hide in long grass.

Zebras have big ears. They move them around to listen for hungry lions.

Every zebra has a different striped pattern.

Zebras have strong teeth, perfect for munching grasses.

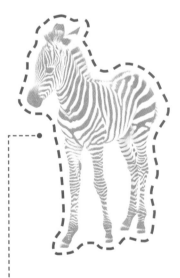

Baby zebras are called **foals**.

Giraffes

Giraffes are the tallest land animals in the world. They use their long necks to reach leaves in tall trees.

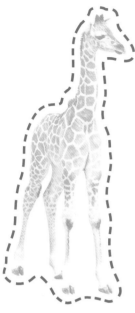

A baby giraffe is called a calf.

A newborn baby giraffe is as tall as a man.

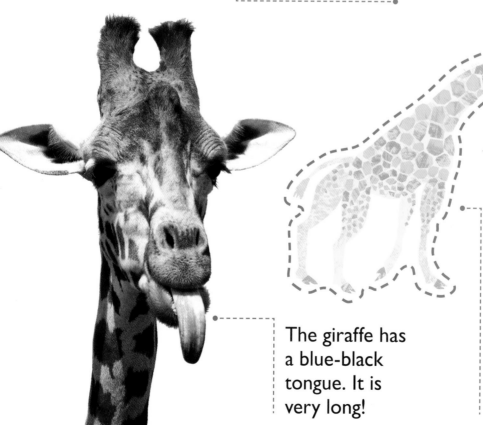

The giraffe has a blue-black tongue. It is very long!

Giraffes can run fast, but they get tired quickly.

33

Big Cats

Did you know?

A group of lions is called a pride.

Big cats are powerful animals. They are strong and fierce and make great hunters.

The tallest cat on the grasslands is the mighty **lion**. It has long, sharp teeth and a powerful bite.

The thick fur around a male lion's head is called a mane.

Baby lions are called cubs.

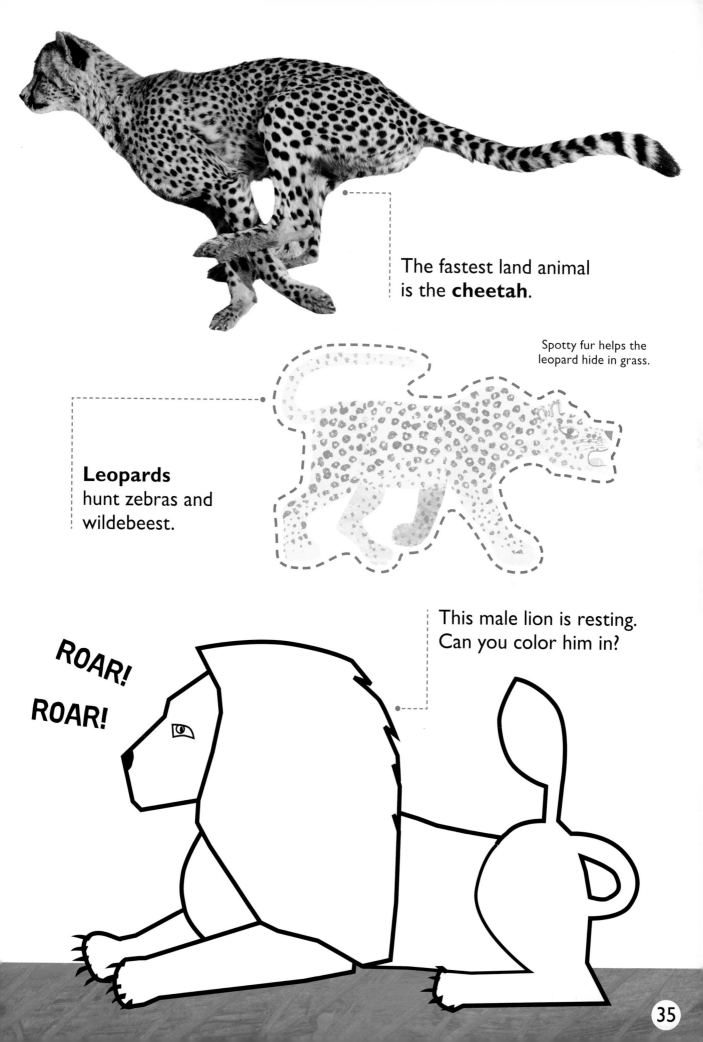

The fastest land animal is the **cheetah**.

Spotty fur helps the leopard hide in grass.

Leopards hunt zebras and wildebeest.

This male lion is resting. Can you color him in?

ROAR!

ROAR!

Vultures and Hyenas

Vultures and **hyenas** are hunters. Hyenas can smell a dead animal from far away. Vultures spot their dinner from the air.

Vultures have bald heads and hooked beaks.

Did you know?

Vultures pee on their legs to cool down!

The **spotted hyena** eats lions' leftovers.

Hyenas sometimes hunt zebra or antelope.

A hyena's bite can crunch through elephant bones.

Honeybees

Honeybees live in hives with lots of other bees. The queen bee is in charge of the hive.

They visit flowers to collect a sugary juice called nectar.

Buzzzzz

The bees turn the nectar into honey and store it in honeycombs.

One bee can only make a tiny amount of honey. It would take lots and lots of bees to make enough honey to fill a jar!

Buzzzzz

The fast flapping of the honeybee's wings is what makes the buzzing sound.

Rhinos

Rhinos have thick skin and one or two horns, which they can use in battles with other rhinos.

Did you know?

They warn other rhinos away with the smell of their poop!

The **white rhinoceros** is the second-largest land mammal. Only elephants are bigger.

A rhino's horns are made out of the same material as our fingernails—keratin.

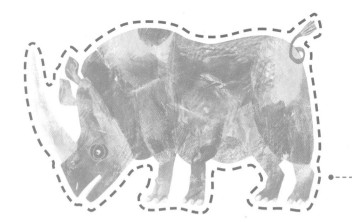

The **black rhinoceros**, like all rhinos, can't see very well. It relies on sounds and smells instead.

The black rhino is slightly smaller than the white rhino.

Rhinos like to roll in mud. It keeps them cool.

Elephants

Elephants are the largest living land animal. They have thick, gray skin and long trunks.

They eat grass and leaves.

An **African elephant's** trunk is as long as a man.

Elephants can suck water into their trunks then blow it out again!

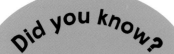

Did you know?
Elephants love to swim and splash in rivers.

Elephants send messages by stamping the ground.

A baby elephant is called a **calf**.

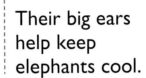

Their big ears help keep elephants cool.

Elephants use mud as sun block. Use your best crayons to cover this elephant in mud!

Watering Holes

Grassland animals visit watering holes to drink and eat. Huge **hippos** and snapping **crocodiles** can be found there.

A hippo has very thick skin.

Hippos' nostrils stick out of the water so they can breathe.

Hippos keep cool in the water during hot days.

Birds peck away insects off the hippo's skin.

Their huge teeth are used for fighting, not eating. They mostly eat grass.

Crocodiles have one of the strongest bites in the animal kingdom.

Crocodiles have scaly skin, long tails, and very sharp teeth!

SNAP!

Crocodiles hide in watering holes, waiting to catch their dinner. They eat fish, birds, and other small animals.

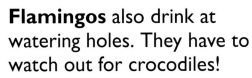

Flamingos are pink because they eat so many pink shrimp!

Flamingos also drink at watering holes. They have to watch out for crocodiles!

On the Prairie

The grasslands of North America are called prairies. They are home to lots of different animals.

The front of a bison is covered in thick, shaggy hair.

The male **bison** uses his huge head to head-butt other males.

The **bobcat** is twice the size of a pet cat. Its favorite food is rabbit.

Screech owls swoop down and use their sharp claws to catch mice.

Did you know?

An owl can fly without making a sound.

An **owl** has large eyes to help it see at night.

A **prairie dog** stands upright on its back legs to look for danger.

Prairie dogs are excellent diggers.

Prairie dogs live in 'towns' of underground tunnels. Some are as large as human towns!

Polar Lands

In the far north and far south of the world, the polar lands are covered with ice and snow for much of the year. They are the coldest places on Earth, but home to some wonderful wild animals.

Seals

Seals are mammals that live mainly in the water, but they also come onto the land.

They have powerful flippers for swimming.

Seals have a layer of fat called blubber under their skin to keep them warm.

They have to come above the water to breathe.

A baby seal drinks its mother's milk until it is old enough to hunt fish.

Baby seals are called pups.

Leopard seals are hunters. They snatch smaller seals and penguins in their jaws.

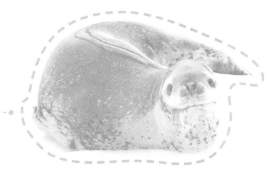

The **southern elephant seal** dives deep to catch fish, holding its breath for a long time.

The southern elephant seal has an inflatable nose!

Can you color in this leopard seal?

Polar Bears

Polar bears rule the Arctic. They are big and strong and can be hard to spot in the white snow.

Their paws have hairy soles to grip the ice.

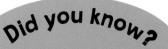

Polar bears hunt and eat seals.

The polar bear has sharp claws that hook onto its prey.

Cubs stay close to their mother for more than two years, learning to swim and hunt.

A baby polar bear is called a cub.

The female walrus has shorter tusks than a male.

The narwhal is a medium-sized whale that also lives in the cold waters of the Arctic.

Narwhals often look like they are sword-fighting with their long tusks.

The male narwhal has a spiral tusk that can grow very long.

Rainforests

Tropical rainforests, or jungles, are hot and wet. There are more kinds of animals and plants in tropical rainforests than anywhere else in the world!

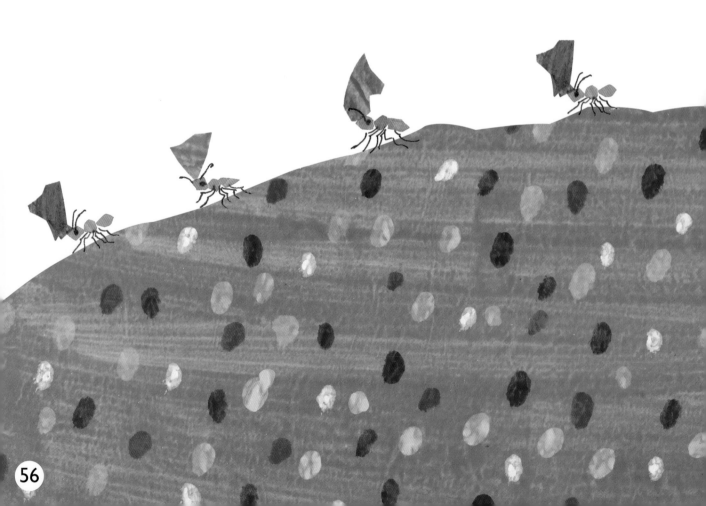

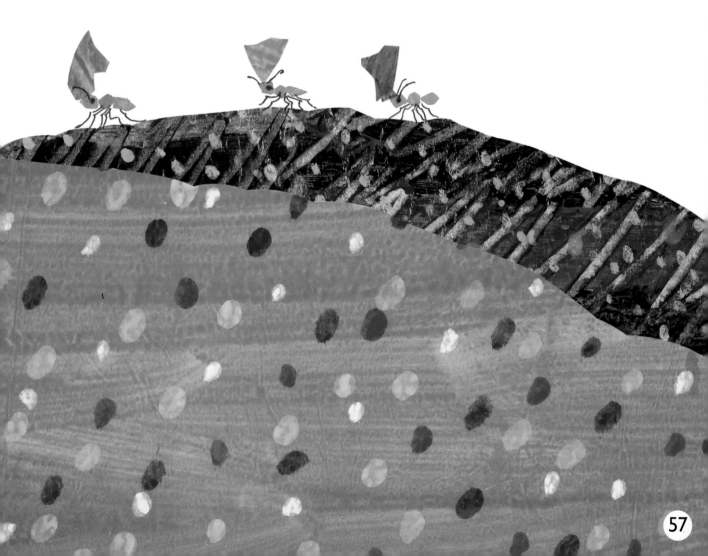

Birds

Bursting with seeds, nuts, berries, and insects, the rainforest is like a restaurant for **birds**!

Parrots brighten up the rainforest with their colorful feathers.

A parrot's hooked beak crushes seeds.

Squawk!

Toucans have huge beaks for reaching fruit to eat.

Some toucans are very noisy! They croak to warn their flock of any danger.

This quetzal has shimmering green feathers.

The beautiful **quetzal** lives in the rainforests of Central America.

Peacocks have an amazing tail of colorful feathers.

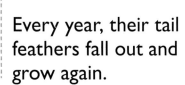

Every year, their tail feathers fall out and grow again.

Did you know?

Peacocks are males. Females are called peahens.

Monkeys

Monkeys are clever animals. They are fun, too—they sometimes play tricks on each other!

Spider monkeys talk to each other using screeches, barks, and other sounds.

Oo Oo Oo!

Their long arms and legs are great for climbing trees.

Can you color in this silly monkey?

Gorillas

Gorillas are a type of ape. They are big and strong, but they mostly like to eat leaves and fruit.

They beat their chests to scare away attackers.

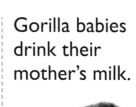

Many gorillas lose their homes when rainforests are cut down for wood or farming.

Gorilla babies drink their mother's milk.

Just like a human, a gorilla has a thumb and four fingers.

Critters

Critters are small animals, like **crickets**, **ants** and **beetles**. They like to live in damp places. The rainforest is bursting with critters!

Click beetles jump in the air and make a loud click to escape from their enemies.

A beetle's front wings form a tough shell.

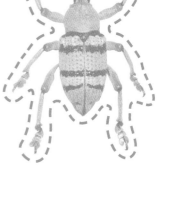

Most insects have two pairs of wings, but sometimes these are hidden.

Did you know?

The titan beetle's jaws are strong enough to break a pencil in half.

The **praying mantis** waits quietly for a bug, then lunges forward to grab it with its front legs.

A **cicada** makes a chirping sound with the drum-like parts of its lower body.

A chirping cicada can be heard from far away.

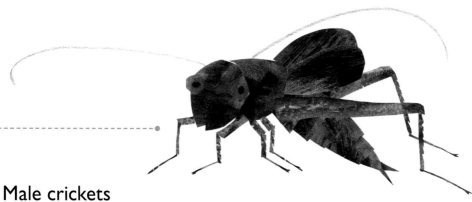

Male crickets chirp to attract a female mate.

Crickets chirp by rubbing their wings together.

CHIRP CHIRP!

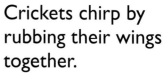

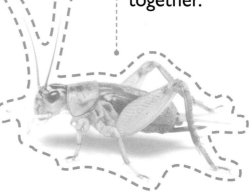

Snakes

These long, scaly reptiles can be found slithering along the rainforest floor or high up in the trees.

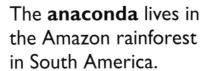

The **emerald tree boa** blends in with the green of the jungle.

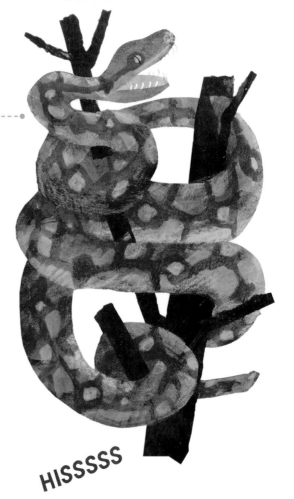

The **anaconda** lives in the Amazon rainforest in South America.

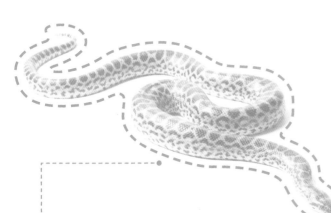

The anaconda is the largest **snake** in the world. It can weigh as much as three adult men.

HISSSSS

Lizards

Lizards are cold-blooded animals that like to be warmed by the sun in the daytime.

Did you know?
Some lizards can break off their tail if they are attacked!

This green iguana has long claws for climbing.

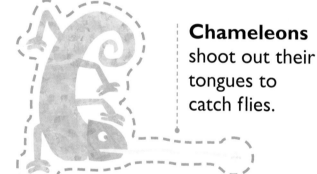

Chameleons shoot out their tongues to catch flies.

Green iguanas spend nearly their whole life in trees.

Chameleons change color to hide in their surroundings.

Chameleons can point their eyes in different directions!

Tigers

Tigers are the largest big cats in the world. They have orange, black, and white striped fur and sharp teeth.

Did you know?
Every tiger has a different pattern of stripes.

Tigers hunt alone.
They often hunt at night.

Roarrrrr!

Tigers use their long front teeth to kill their prey.

They only roar to communicate with other tigers. They don't roar at other animals.

Tigers are completely blind for the first week of their life.

Jaguars and Black Panthers

Jaguars and **black panthers** both have strong jaws and claws. A jaguar has spots, but a black panther's markings are hard to see because its fur is dark.

Like tigers, jaguars prefer to hunt on their own.

Jaguars hunt deer and other small mammals.

A black panther's long tail helps it to balance.

The black panther blends into the shade of the jungle.

Fireflies and Glowworms

Fireflies and **glowworms** light up the rainforest with their amazing glows of color.

A firefly is a type of beetle that glows in the dark to attract a mate.

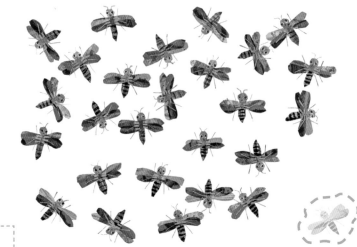

Their light can be yellow, green, or orange.

Firefly eggs hatch into tiny glowing larvae called glowworms.

Can you color in this firefly? Don't forget the glowing tip on its tail.

Bats

Most **bats** are nocturnal. This means they sleep in the day and wake up at night.

Bats squeak then listen for echoes in the dark to find their way around.

Some bats only eat fruit, like bananas and mangoes. They are called **fruit bats**.

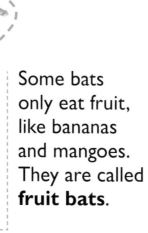

SQUEAK!

Did you know?
Bats sleep upside down.

Bats use their wings to fly and to hold food to eat.

Deserts

Deserts are rocky or sandy places that
can be very, very hot. With little rainfall,
they are the driest places on Earth,
but some animals manage to survive there.

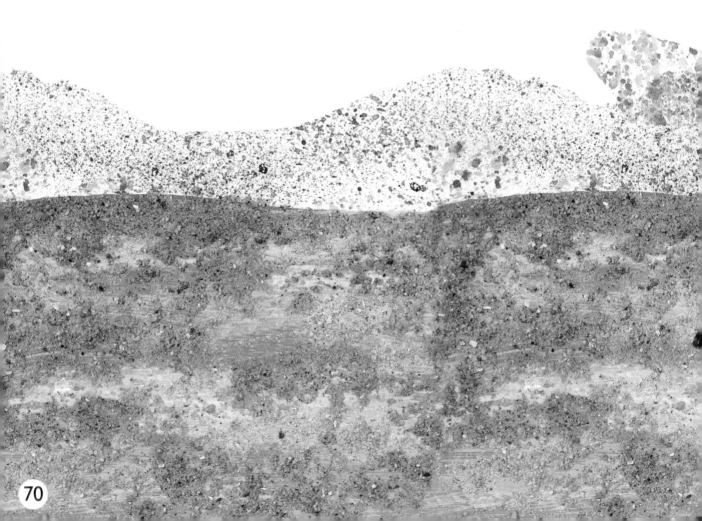

Camels

Camels have one or two humps on their back. Camels are well-suited to hot, dusty deserts—their wide feet help them to walk in the sand.

A camel can survive on the fat in its hump for several months without eating.

They have long eyelashes to keep sand from getting in their eyes.

Camels provide transportation for people and goods across desert lands.

Desert Reptiles

The desert is home to reptiles such as **snakes**, **lizards**, and **tortoises**.

This is a **gila monster**. It is one of the biggest lizards in the desert.

It has sharp teeth and a poisonous bite.

Desert tortoises spend almost all of their time in burrows underground.

They can live for more than 50 years!

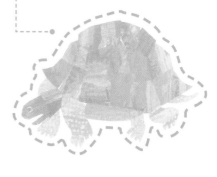

Wide, thick feet help the tortoise to dig in the sand.

Kangaroos

Kangaroos have four legs but are fastest when hopping on two!

The largest kangaroo is the **red kangaroo**. It can weigh as much as a baby elephant.

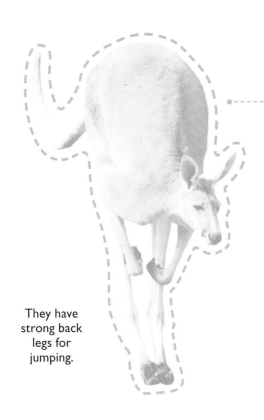

The long tail is useful for balance.

They have strong back legs for jumping.

They can leap almost 10 yards in one hop!

A kangaroo mother gives birth to a tiny baby called a joey that grows inside a pouch on her tummy.

'Boxing matches' sometimes take place between male kangaroos.

Red kangaroos look for food in the cool of the night. They eat grass and leaves.

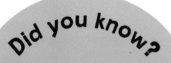
Did you know?

Kangaroos can't hop backward— their tails would get in the way!

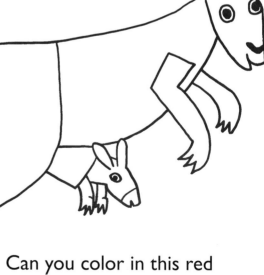

Can you color in this red kangaroo and her joey?

Eagles and Owls

Eagles and owls are great hunters, always ready to swoop down on a lizard or a rat.

The **golden eagle** is one of the largest eagles in the world.

The **burrowing owl** keeps cool underground. It copies the sound of a rattlesnake to keep safe from danger.

The **elf owl** is tiny. It's the height of a soft drink can.

Locusts

Locusts are grasshoppers that have gathered together to form a huge group or a swarm.

A grasshopper's ears are on its belly.

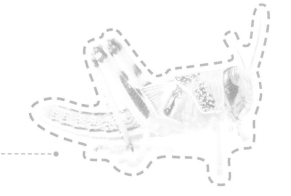

Grasshoppers have strong back legs for hopping and two pairs of wings for flying.

A swarm of locusts can eat all of a farmer's crops.

Did you know?
The largest swarm ever recorded was made up of trillions of locusts!

Mule Deer

Mule deer eat desert plants and flowers. They live together in large groups called herds.

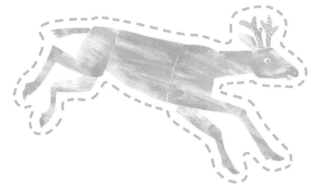

They are most active early in the morning and at night, when the desert is cool.

Did you know?

Mule deer can run, but they usually leap.

Male mule deer clash antlers to show off to female deer.

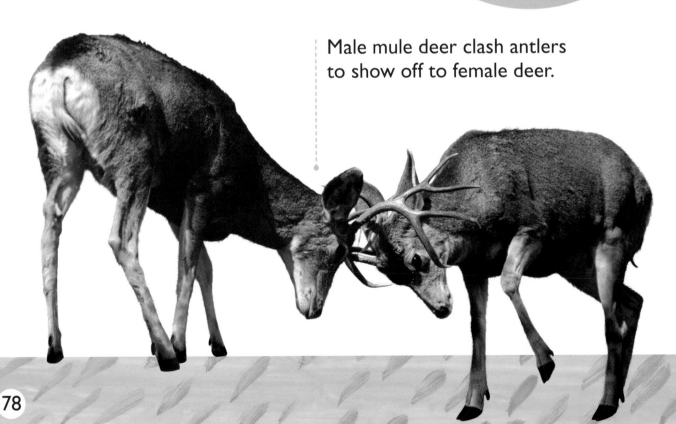

Rattlesnakes

Rattlesnakes make a rattling noise with the tips of their tails. This noise scares off hunters.

RATTLE
RATTLE

Rattlesnakes eat small animals such as birds, mice, and lizards.

A rattlesnake has a poisonous bite.

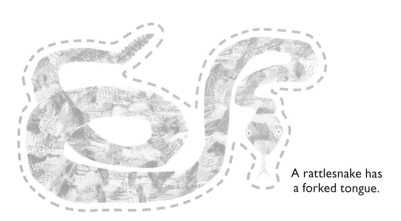

A rattlesnake has a forked tongue.

Herons land near ponds in search of fish to eat.

Herons have long, pointed beaks for catching fish.

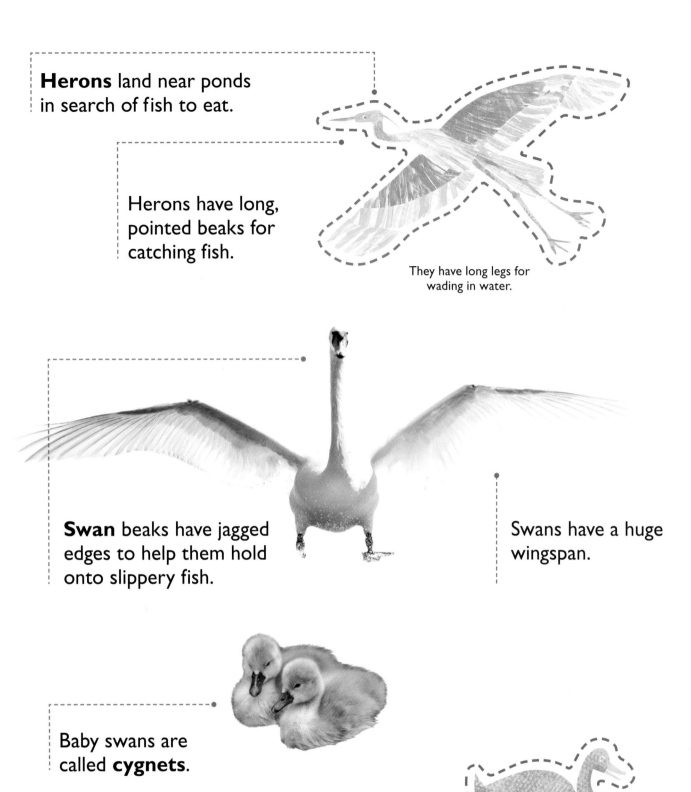

They have long legs for wading in water.

Swan beaks have jagged edges to help them hold onto slippery fish.

Swans have a huge wingspan.

Baby swans are called **cygnets**.

Duck feathers are covered in an oil that makes them waterproof.

Ducks and swans have wide, webbed feet for paddling.

Ladybugs

A **ladybug** is a small beetle, usually with red front wings covered in black spots.

Like all insects, ladybugs have six legs.

Ladybugs have wings so they can fly.

Ladybugs can have lots of spots or none at all.

Ladybugs eat little green bugs called aphids. They can eat as many as 50 in one day.

Spiders

Spiders have eight legs. They make beautiful webs to catch flies.

This is a garden spider.

A spider's web is made from silk from their bodies.

Flies get stuck in their webs. Spiders then wrap up the flies in silk and eat them up!

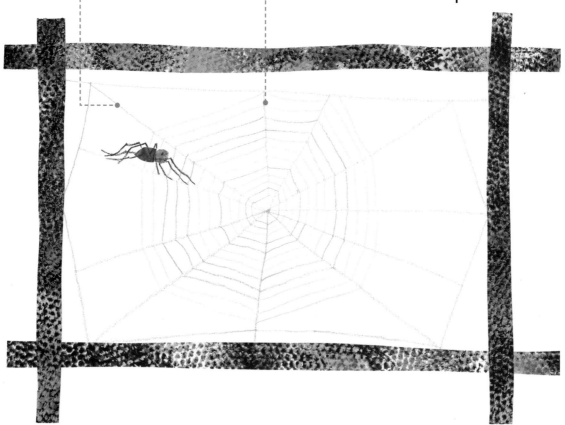

Horses

Horses are big, strong animals. They live in stables and eat lots of grass and hay.

Did you know?
Horses can sleep standing up!

People use saddles and stirrups to ride horses.

A horse has long, strong legs that are perfect for running fast!

The hair down a horse's neck is called a mane.

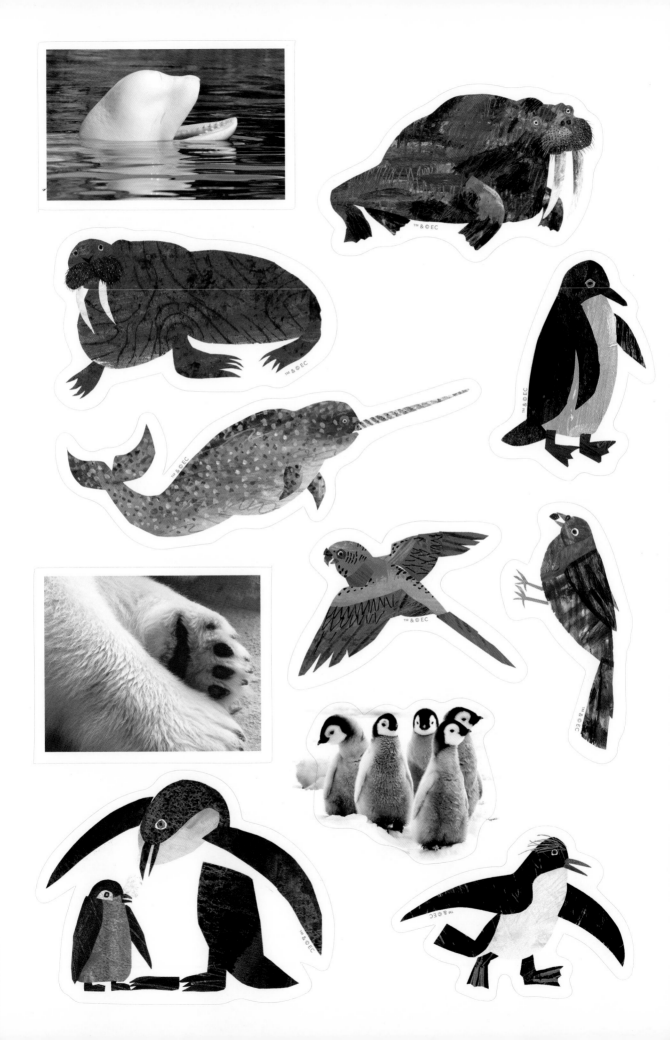

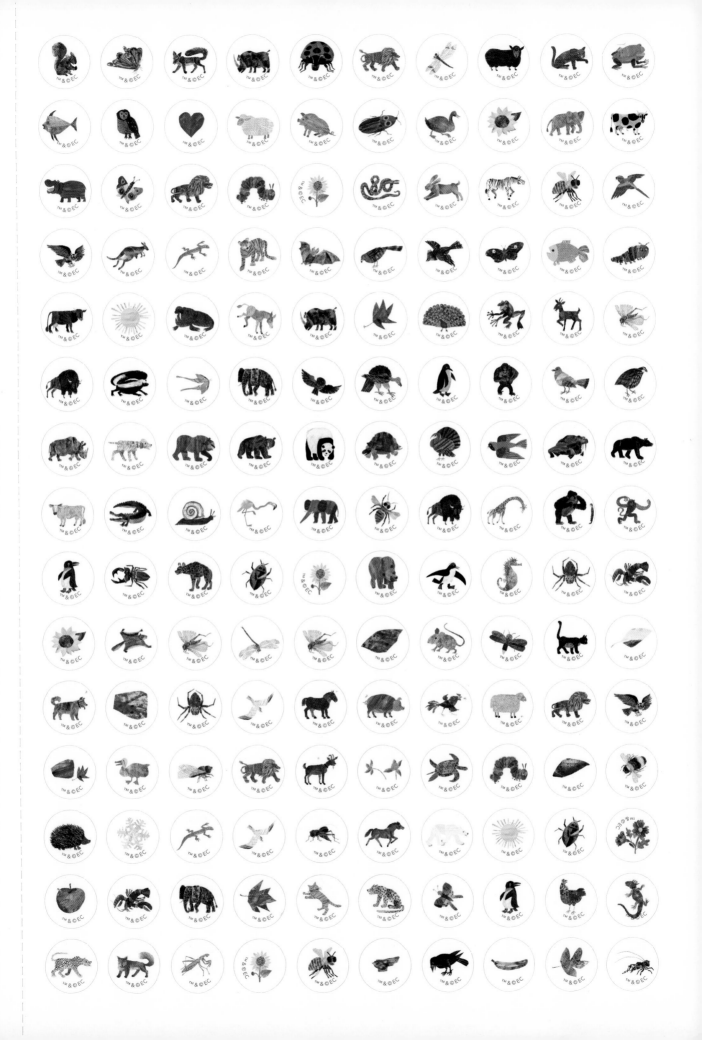

froglet

tadpole

frogspawn

frog